Dejah & Summer
In The Time of Magic

Books by Warren Bluhm

Dejah & Summer In The Time of Magic

Ebenezer: A Sequel of Sorts to A Christmas Carol

96 flashes

Myke Phoenix

The Imaginary Revolution

The Imaginary Bomb

+ + + + +

War IS the Crime

It's Going to be All Right

Echoes of Freedom Past

Full: Rockets, Bells & Poetry

Gladness is Infectious

How to Play a Blue Guitar

A Bridge at Crossroads

A Scream of Consciousness

Refuse to be Afraid

Wordsmith and podcaster, Warren Bluhm is a reporter, editor and storyteller who lives near the shores of Green Bay with his golden retrievers, Dejah and Summer.

Summer & Dejah In The Time of Magic

A Halloween Fantasy

Warren Bluhm

www.warrenbluhm.com

SUMMER & DEJAH IN THE TIME OF MAGIC

A Halloween Fantasy

© 2024 Warren Bluhm

ISBN 979-8-9863331-8-2

For Mom

Chapter 1
An Adventure Begins

On this glorious morning I stood on the deck and cried, "It's a good day to have a good day!" but did I believe it? The sun had not yet risen and there was an October chill in the air. Still, I was rested from a longer night's sleep than usual, if stiff from the inactivity. What adventures might lay ahead for me and this young patient hound at my side, with her old compatriot panting across the room? Were our greatest adventures behind us, after all, and we were fated to live out our days pacing among these cluttered rooms, sifting through the debris of old books and forgotten papers?

"No!" I cried, and not just because the young dog had begun to harass her older sister. "No, I refuse to settle into a routine that leads to my death bed. There are years ahead that I mean to navigate, perhaps even circumnavigate, worlds to explore, sights to see, aromas to breathe in, perhaps even pleasures to touch. I may be moving more slowly, but I'm not dead yet." From the corner of my mind emerged the melody of a long-forgotten tune, and I tasted the memory of a fine meal, to complete the journey of all five senses. "This is life, and I mean to live," I murmured.

As if in agreement, the aging dog shifted from one side of the love seat to the side closer to me, and looked at me expectantly.

"What would you have me do?" I asked. "I fed you, I let you out —"

"What were you just talking about, silly?" the old dog said, and I gasped, because she had never spoken in 11 years. "Adventure! Let's have an adventure!"

Of course, I wanted to shout, "You talked! You're talking! How can it be that you're talking?"

But instead I said, rather meekly, "What kind of adventure were you thinking about?"

I would swear that her panting shifted in a way that made it sound like she was laughing.

"The kind of adventure that begins with your dog talking to you, of course," she said. "That's the elephant in the room, isn't it?"

"Oh my gosh," I said. "Is this the beginning of another book that I'll never finish?"

"There you go again," the dog sighed. "Let's just start the adventure and see where it leads."

"All right, I guess I'm game," I said. "What should we do first?"

"Let's go back into the back yard," said the old dog. "Did I mention that when we went out to do our business, we noticed an inter-dimensional portal hovering near the garden shed?"

"You most certainly did not!"

"Well," she said, "I most certainly just did."

The younger dog whined, but I slid the patio door open.

Chapter 2
The Portal

"Eww, you need to pick up back here more," said Summer, who was the timid young dog.

"I'll take care of it after we deal with this inter-dimensional portal that Dejah found near the garden shed," I said, watching my step anyway.

"It's right over here," Dejah said.

"I'm still a little freaked out that you're talking," I admitted.

"That freaks you out, but not the inter-dimensional portal floating in the air?" Dejah said.

"Well, I have to say that adds to the freakout factor."

We reached the garden shed. Sure enough, some sort of round glowing thing was hanging in the air, kind of a cross between the Guardian of Forever in Star Trek and the Stargate in Stargate except without the artificial structure forming it, and we could see another world through it. Not an alien world — we could see grass and trees on the other side — just a different world.

"Hang on," Dejah said, looking up through the portal. "What's that?"

"I don't see anything."

"That's because you're not looking from down here."

Then I saw what she meant. A shadow fell across the opening, and then a huge, scaly foot appeared. It was ghastly and gnarled and looked more like a tree trunk than animal skin, with three clawed toes.

The foot began a cautious descent through the portal into the back yard.

"I'm going back in the house now," said Summer, and she scampered up the stairs to the deck.

I held my breath, wondering if the creature was flexible enough to fold itself through the portal. And if it could, was it friend or foe? Just because the foot was incredibly ugly didn't mean the beast had ugly intent, right? Still, I wish I had thought to bring a baseball bat.

The foot reached the ground and landed on a fairly squishy bit of dog poop.

We heard an unearthly sound, a cry that chilled me to the bone, after the foot turned to make its bottom visible to the creature on the other side of the portal.

The best approximation of the sound we heard is something like, "EEEWWWWWWW." The foot quickly lifted back to the other side of the portal, which then shrank suddenly into nonexistence with a decided "Pop!"

For a moment there was no sound except Dejah's panting.

"Well, that was interesting," she said then.

"I told you that you needed to pick up back here!" Summer called from the deck.

"We just fended off an alien invasion!" I said, defensively.

"Or ruined an opportunity for first contact," Dejah said. When I looked at her curiously, she added, "Hey, I watch Star Trek, too, when you do. You think all I do is nap down here?"

"OK, OK, I'll go get the pooper scooper," I said.

"That will have to wait," said Dejah. "Look behind you."

I turned, and at first I broke into a delighted smile, but a corner of my mind was terrified.

Chapter 3
Elf Quest

Was it a leprechaun? A hobbit? Whatever it was, it was not of this world.

"What are you looking at?" said the little person.

"Why, we're looking at you," said Dejah, as I was still speechless. "You're not from around here, are you?"

"I might say the same of you," the newcomer said. "We've lived here forever, minding our business, and you come along and build that monstrous wooden cave on the side of the hill, pushing us all back in the woods and putting up fences."

He — she? — was cute as a button, with a smooth childlike face but an adult voice, very much like a Wendy Pini elf or the Lucky Charms spokesman. If I had to guess, I would say it seemed more hurt than angry, but the voice carried a bit of both emotions.

"We've been here for 12 years. I never saw anyone like you before," I said.

"Bulldozers, concrete and wood barriers, lawn mowers tearing down all the plant life — and the dogs chasing all the squirrels and rabbits — you think we feel welcome to come visit?" said the elf.

"Gosh, I'm sorry, really I am," I said. "I guess we didn't think we might be uprooting someone's home."

"You didn't think — that's a real good way of putting it," said the elf, and now there was definitely more anger than hurt. "It's obvious you didn't think."

There was an awkward silence, and Summer came slowly down the stairs from the deck, walked up and sniffed the elf's hair.

"What do you think you're doing?" he or she snapped.

"That's a really nice-smelling shampoo," Summer said. "It's like the smell of springtime."

"I don't use a shampoo," the elf muttered. "That's just the smell of me."

"Well, you smell nice," Summer said. "I'm sorry we chase the squirrels. They say mean things to us."

"You'd say mean things, too, if they chopped down all the trees with your nests and put up their own homes instead."

"Good point," Dejah said. "How can we make it up to you?"

"You can't," said the elf. "The trees won't grow back, and anyway this was 10 years ago. It's too late."

"Twelve years, actually," I said. "I wish we'd been more careful."

"Meh, at least you built here on the edge of the land instead of way back in the woods like some of your people do," the elf conceded. I decided not to tell him we thought about building a second house in the woods but never got around to it.

"Maybe we can be friends from now on," Summer suggested. "We can promise not to chase the squirrels if they'll stop being mean. I already leave the rabbits alone."

"Yeah, why is that?" I asked.

Summer tilted her head. "They're so cute."

The elf looked thoughtful. "A friendship with the human ravagers? That's a pretty hard sell for my people, but if you're serious —"

Just then we all heard a high-pitched screech from up above. It was the cry of an eagle seeking its prey, and it was coming down fast towards us.

Chapter 4
Talons of the Eagle

An eagle is a majestic creature that makes a breathtaking sight when it is navigating the eddies of a gentle breeze. I have to say, however, that seeing it diving toward you at full speed can be a little disconcerting.

I didn't think it was going to try to carry off a golden retriever or a portly human. On the other hand, I figured our new friend the elf might appear to be a tasty morsel to a bird of prey.

But before I could make a move to protect him or her, the little person waved a hand and a shield of some sort appeared in his/her hand. Just as suddenly, in a voice louder than a dog's bark and — in fact — louder than my own loudest shout, the elf cried, "BACK OFF, BUDDY!"

Talons extended to the fullest, the startled eagle suddenly waved its wings in a sudden stop and diverted to the top of the backyard fence. It quickly regained its dignity and drew itself up officiously.

"I beg your pardon," the eagle said. "You obviously have no idea who I am."

"You're a bald eagle, who knows, maybe you're the local king of the bald eagles," said the little being. "Big hairy deal."

"How dare you!" cried the mighty bird.

"How? It's easy. You're nothing special, just a bird that likes to try to intimidate innocents," the elf said in a huff. "I've seen mooks like you picking at roadkill like any other buzzard. You don't scare me."

"You ought to be scared," snarled the eagle. "I could have you for lunch."

"Can we not talk about dining on sentient beings?" Dejah asked in a can't-we-just-get-along tone. "Clearly we've gotten off on the wrong foot, and maybe we can start by introducing ourselves. I'm Dejah, my counterpart here is named Summer, and the large human is —"

"Not in the mood," said the eagle. "If you're going to resist being eaten, I'll just head somewhere with more willing victims."

"Guy's got a future in politics," the elf said under his/her breath as the big bird flew officiously away.

"I have a question," I said. "In the last few minutes, an inter-dimensional portal has opened and closed, we met an elfin being who accused us of destroying his ancestral home, and we've insulted a bald eagle who was hoping to eat the elf for lunch."

"Yep," said Summer.

"Oh, that's another thing," I said. "My dogs are talking to me."

"We certainly are," Dejah agreed.

"So can someone explain to me what the bejeebers is going on around here?" I said, rather earnestly.

At precisely that moment, a sound like thunder rumbled the ground, and a pillar of fire shot into the sky from the other side of the backyard fence.

"Oh, great," said the elf. "The dragon's here."

Chapter 5

A dragon in the yard

"Hi guys," a booming voice boomed. "What's shaking?"

"Besides the house, you mean?" Dejah asked.

The dragon was enormous. It — well, you know what a dragon looks like. It's almost a cliche now. Long head and snout like a giraffe's only all scaly, four legs and enormous wings that fold against its back, long pointy tail, claws — you know the drill. And of course, a deep voice that sounds menacing even when it says, "Hi guys, what's shaking?"

Dejah didn't seem to be particularly rattled, but Summer scampered up on the deck and seemed miffed that I'd closed the patio door.

"Yo, Seth," said the little elfin being. "Haven't seen you around for awhile."

"Been busy, here and there," said Seth the Dragon, and then turned to me. "Did you see an inter-dimensional portal around here somewhere? I thought I sensed a disturbance in the calm a few minutes ago."

"You're talking to me?"

"Well, you're the only one there."

"Right, I got a dragon in my yard quoting Travis Bickle," I murmured, "as if this all wasn't weird enough."

"Great movie. A little dark for my tastes," said the dragon. "So did you see an inter-dimensional portal or not?"

"We did!" piped up Dejah.

"No offense, lady, but I'm talking to the human," Seth said. "Humans usually can't see portals like we can."

"Apologies," Dejah said.

"No worries," said the dragon, then looked at me with those big dark eyes, and his nostrils flared a little. "So?"

"Yes!" I said a bit too quickly, then took a breath and repeated, "Yes. I saw the portal."

"How about that, Grenn? The plot thickens," Seth said, turning to the elf.

"He can see me, too. It's a little too spot-on to the prophecy for my comfort," replied the elf. So his (?) name was Grenn.

"What plot? What prophecy?" Summer asked from the deck. The poor thing sounded as scared as when the neighbors down by the shore set off fireworks over the bay.

The elfin being and the dragon exchanged a "how much should we tell them" kind of look.

"We don't want to alarm you," said the dragon in as kindly a tone as he could muster with his inevitably menacing voice.

"Too late! We're alarmed!!" Summer yelped.

"Speak for yourself," said Dejah. "This is pretty interesting."

"Let me have it," I said. "Just be gentle."

Grenn and Seth sighed. At least it looked like the elf sighed; when a dragon sighs, you can't really hear anything else.

"October is the month of magic," Grenn said. "You humans are more likely to see elves and dragons and other creatures of the other worlds when the leaves begin to turn and the air begins to cool. It's just how it is."

"But apparently this morning is a little unusual even for October," I said.

"I don't want to be Captain Obvious, but you and I have been having a conversation," said Dejah, her English cream golden retriever eyes rolling.

"Like I said, this is unusual," I said.

"Yes, it is," said Seth the Dragon. "And there's this prophecy —"

At that Grenn's eyes began to glow and his voice grew larger than his little elf self again.

"In the time of magic there will come a day when the dimensions merge and tongues are unlocked to a human," Grenn intoned. "Be on watch against the Evil One on that day, lest it consume all in its path."

"The Evil One? You mean like Satan?" I asked.

The elf shrugged. "That's as good a name as any."

"OK, the portal and the talking dogs and the little elf-guy and the talking eagle are all signs that we need to watch out for the Evil One?"

"Pretty much," the dragon said. "But we're OK so far. It always announces its arrival with the Chime of Doom."

As if on cue came the thunderous clang of a bell overhead, as if from a mutant Liberty Bell a hundred times larger than the original.

And on the other side of the fence, next to the dragon, an inter-dimensional portal reappeared.

Chapter 6

That worblatt in the window

"I don't think our 'secret weapon' will work this time," Dejah said ruefully.

Sure enough, as before, a huge, scaly foot began to emerge from the portal. It was still ghastly, still gnarled, and still looked more like a tree trunk than animal skin, with three clawed toes.

And this time, when it reached the ground, the foot found purchase, not dog poop. And then, a second foot came through.

"The Evil One, I presume?" I said, and suddenly realized that Grenn the elfin being was no longer in sight. "Oh! Should we run?"

"Get in the house," said Seth the Dragon. "I'll handle this."

I made my way to the stairs, checked the bottom of my shoes, climbed up and looked back. Seth had unfurled his wings and reared back on his hind legs. Dejah was underneath him, staring at the spectacle.

"DEJAH!" I screamed. She looked up at me and blinked.

"Oh, dear. Coming!" she said and scampered to the deck as quickly as an 11-year-old golden retriever is able.

Summer dashed inside as soon as I slid the patio door open, and Dejah waddled in behind. As soon as I got the door closed, we heard a humungous whooshing sound and the daylight grew brighter outside.

I ran over to the living room windows facing the back yard and saw Seth the Dragon standing at the fence. Whatever came through the portal was huge, perhaps 20 feet high and almost as wide.

Sadly, I had no idea what the creature looked like in its prime, because all that remained was a 20-foot-high pile of blackened ash. Seth took a deep breath and blew, and the ash dispersed across the septic mound on the other side of the fence.

"It's OK," the dragon called. "Show's over."

"I missed the whole thing," Summer said.

"Me, too, it was pretty quick," I admitted. I opened the patio door and yelled, "Isn't the portal still open?"

"Yeah, but worblatts don't run in packs," Seth said. "There won't be another one of those things coming through anytime soon."

Grenn reappeared next to the garden shed.

"That was a big one," he said.

"Yep," was all Seth said in reply.

"What else is on the other side of that portal?" I asked.

"Wanna see?" Grenn asked.

"No!" Summer cried.

"If it's all the same to you," I said, "I'd prefer to stay on this side of the portal."

Dejah rumbled down the stairs, went to the fence and sniffed in the direction of the blackened ash.

"I'm surprised that something called the Evil One isn't more durable," she said, perhaps a little too haughtily.

"That's because the Evil One isn't a worblatt," said the elfin one.

"What?" Dejah looked a tad surprised. "I though that big bell sound was the Chime of Doom."

"Right, it was," agreed Seth the Dragon. "That just means the Evil One is in the neighborhood with a minion or two."

"Or three," agreed Seth.

"Or four?!" I asked warily.

Seth and Grenn looked at each other. "No," the dragon said finally. "I don't think I've ever seen him with more than three minions."

Summer ventured out onto the deck at last and stood as close to my knees as she could without tipping me over. "I thought you said there wouldn't be any more creatures coming through the portal?"

"No more worblatts, for now," Grenn said. "That much is true. But —"

Just then, a buzzing sound came from the inter-dimensional portal, and a second later a swarm of insects surged through.

Chapter 7
What Goes On

The bugs were a black, undulating cloud. I stepped back and raised my hands to wave them away, but I realized almost at once that they were somehow familiar. With a start I recognized that they were —

"Lake flies!" Grenn screamed, waving his arms blindly about his face and turning in a circle as the little beasts swarmed past and around him.

"But lake flies are harmless," I cried.

"Of course they are!" the elf yelled. "But they're infernally annoying!!"

Every year, three or four times for a couple of days at a time, a new hatch of lake flies hatches and harasses folks all over this neck of the woods. They don't sting, they don't bite, they don't menace anyone or anything, they just fly around, gather around light sources, and make a general nuisance. As far as anyone knows, they don't serve any purpose except to provide a food source for the birds, irritate humans, and commit mass suicide against windshields all along the highway.

"Why would a swarm of lake flies come through the evil inter-dimensional portal?" Dejah inquired.

"Portals aren't good or evil," said Seth the Dragon. "They're just entryways between dimensions. There's good and evil on either side."

"I think lake flies are evil," Summer said.

"No, silly, they're just infernally annoying, like Grenn said," Dejah replied.

"Seth!" Grenn shouted, waving his hands madly. "A little help here?!"

"Oh, sure," Seth said. The dragon unfurled his wings again and beat them furiously. Well, maybe *furiously* is the wrong word, because he wasn't really furious. Perhaps he beat his wings vigorously, but in any case the lake flies were dispersed after a few seconds. The undulating black cloud reconnoitered over the big field next to our house.

"Now that we have a moment, could you guys explain a little more about what's going on around here?" I asked. "Who made this prophecy that animals would start talking and the Evil One would come calling?"

"The elves," said the dragon.

"The dragons," said the elf.

They looked at each other.

"I thought it was part of your culture," Seth said.

"I thought it was part of *your* culture," Grenn said.

"Maybe it's an eagle legend," Dejah said, referring to the majestic bird that had visited a few minutes before.

"But in any case, there's a prophecy that animals talking to humans would signal a merging of dimensions and the Evil One showing up to try to destroy everything," I said.

"That's the gist," Grenn said.

"Why would this Evil One want to destroy everything?" Summer asked.

"WHO WANTS TO KNOW?" asked a voice that seemed to come from everywhere at once.

Chapter 8
A good question

"Get behind me, girls," I said bravely, although I wasn't feeling very brave. Dejah got behind me. Summer was still up on the deck and kept glancing at the patio door as if I might have miraculously found a way to open it from where I was standing down below.

My late wife and I named this land Serenity Valley, after the place where a fateful battle happened in the opening minutes of the TV show *Firefly*. Shortly after I lost her, I thought of calling our little three-acre estate Three Willows, after the three sticks we put in the ground a dozen years ago that have grown into huge weeping willow trees that tower overhead. Now I call it Three Willows at Serenity Valley, to cleverly incorporate both names.

I mention those trees because the apparition that appeared now was taller than those trees, taller than the 20-foot-tall worblatt that Seth the Dragon had incinerated before I had a chance to see what it looked like.

He kind of looked like Adonis from the original *Star Trek* series, except he wasn't blond and he wasn't wearing a toga. OK, he only reminded me of Adonis because he was taller than everything. He actually looked like Thanos from the Avengers movies, only he didn't have purple skin or grooves in his chin.

"*This* is the Evil One, I presume," I said to no one in particular.

"Good guess," Seth said.

"WHO ASKED THAT QUESTION?"

"Please, sir," came a plaintive voice from the deck that sounded a lot like Dorothy addressing Oz the Great and Powerful, although we all knew it was actually Summer, my 3-year-old golden retriever. "I was just wondering why you would want to destroy everything."

"BECAUSE I WANT TO!" thundered the voice that seemed to be coming from everywhere at once.

"But why?!" Summer asked sincerely, if timidly.

"BECAUSE IT'S WHAT THE WORLD EXPECTS FROM THE EVIL ONE!" shouted the Evil One with a grim smile.

"Do you always do what the world expects?" asked Dejah. "If the world expected you to jump off a cliff, would you do it?"

"Shush! Shush!" whispered Grenn the elf. "Don't antagonize him."

"I'm not trying to antagonize him," Dejah replied. "I'm asking a question."

"YOU ASK A GOOD QUESTION," the Evil One said, to everyone's surprise. "WHY SHOULD I DESTROY EVERYTHING JUST BECAUSE YOU THINK I WILL?"

"That's what I was asking," Summer said, starting to scratch at the patio door as if her paws might be able to move it.

"STAY HERE," said the monstrous apparition. "I'M GOING TO GO PONDER THIS FOR AWHILE. PERHAPS I WILL SPARE EVERYTHING JUST TO SPITE YOU."

"That would be lovely," Dejah said, but the monster turned suddenly and snapped at her.

"I SAID PERHAPS!" said the Evil One. "I STILL HAVE A TRAGIC BACKSTORY THAT MADE ME THE WAY I AM TODAY, AND PERHAPS I WILL FULFILL MY DESTINY TO END THIS PATHETIC WORLD AFTER ALL. BUT FIRST, I WILL PONDER."

"Ponder away, friend," Seth said.

"I AM NOT YOUR FRIEND! BELLZY, BUB, STAY HERE AND WATCH THE PORTAL."

Two worblatts stepped forward as the Evil One disappeared in a flaming puff of smoke that provided another callback to *The Wizard of Oz*.

"I thought you said worblatts are loners who don't travel together," I said.

"It appears I was mistaken," the dragon admitted.

"This is going to be fun," grinned the worblatt on the left.

Chapter 9

Bellzy and Bub

After seeing only worblatt feet before this — you may recall I described them as huge, scaly feet that were ghastly and gnarled and looked more like a tree trunk than animal skin, with three clawed toes each — it was interesting (albeit a tad horrifying) to see what the rest of a worblatt looked like.

They were each in the neighborhood of 20 feet tall, ghastly and gnarled all the way up, with faces not unlike the crabby apple trees in *The Wizard of Oz* except they were perched atop more conventional necks rather than in the middle of their trunks — and "trunks" is an appropriate word since they did resemble gnarly trees except that they had two legs and two arms.

"Which one of you is Bellzy, and which is Bub?" Dejah asked, craning her neck near the fence line.

"I'm Bellzy," said the one on the right. "He's Bub."

"Why did you say this is going to be fun?" my 11-year-old retriever asked with what sounded like genuine curiosity.

"We've never eaten dog or human before," Bub said. He talked slow but did not appear to be stupid.

"I truly hate to disappoint you, fellers, but you're not eating any dogs or humans today," said Seth the Dragon, and to emphasize the point he blew puffs of smoke out of his nostrils.

"That's very kind of you," Summer said. "Daddy, could you let me in the house, please?" She was still standing on the deck in front of the patio door.

"No one is going anywhere," Bellzy said. He cracked his knuckles and it sounded sort of like a tree falling in the forest. "The boss said to keep an eye on youse."

"Right, he's off somewhere pondering why he wants to destroy all of creation," said Grenn the elfin one. "Who would have thought a puppy's question could throw him into an existential crisis?"

"He's not having a crisis, existential or otherwise," Bub said.

"Sez you," Seth said. "You have to admit, it's odd the Evil One would hesitate to destroy everything when he has the chance, given the prophecy and all that."

"Maybe the Evil One is not as evil as his reputation makes him sound," I said.

"Wait just a gull-darned moment," Bellzy said. "Nobody is as evil as the Evil One. Why do you think they call him the Evil One?"

"We're starting to wonder," said Grenn.

"This is getting ridiculous," said Bub.

"He seems evil enough to me," Summer said from the top of the deck.

"There, you see?" Bub said.

"But why does he have to take any time to think about why he wants to destroy everything?" Dejah asked.

"He thinks about everything," Bellzy said. "He's a very thoughtful personification of evil itself."

"Back to the subject at hand," said Seth the Dragon. "What's to stop me from using you guys as firewood like the last worblatt who stood where you'e standing?"

At this Bellzy and Bub looked stricken, or offended, or whatever worblatts look like when insulted.

"What have we done to deserve such a fate?" asked Bellzy.

"You're working for the Evil One and said something about eating us," said Summer.

"She's got a point, Belz," said Bub.

"Excuse me," came an altogether new voice from the other side of the yard. Those of us who were facing the worblatts whirled. The worblatts themselves just widened their eyes in shock.

Everyone gasped.

Chapter 10

The Crowd Grows Larger

"I did not see this coming," said Grenn the elf.

"We're very good at moving quietly," said the owner of the voice.

Standing at the edge of the woods, just over the septic mound from the 20-foot-high worblatts, was a white-tailed deer.

He was a huge buck, with a rack of antlers that would make him quite a target once deer hunting began in six weeks, and he was accompanied by a doe and two adorable fawns. To complete the Disneyesque image, three gray rabbits hopped along by their feet.

It was so breathtakingly beautiful, I almost forgot that we seemed to be in mortal danger.

"You're not going to chase the bunnies?" I asked Summer and Dejah. The golden retrievers tilted their heads at me.

"Bunnies are too cute to chase," Summer said.

"Good thing they're not S-Q-U-I-R-R-E-L-S," I said.

"Not fair. You know we can't spell," Dejah said, a bit indignantly.

"There seems to be some sort of commotion going on around here," said the great buck.

"You noticed," said Seth the Dragon.

"You should move along," said Bellzy the worblatt. "There's nothing to see here."

"That's not exactly true," said the doe. "I see a human who seems to understand what everyone is saying, a dragon, an elf, two dogs, two worblatts, and a fenced-in yard that could use some waste disposal maintenance."

"I know, right?" said Bub the worblatt. "It's downright icky."

"Thank you," Summer said up on the deck, and then, to me, "I wish you would do something about that."

"Hey, I have a day job, I get tired, I'm sorry," I said. "I'll take care of it tomorrow."

"I saw an eagle, too, Mom! It flew overhead a few minutes ago," one of the fawns said.

"You called her Mom?" Dejah said. "We knew someone named Mom. She left home about a year and a half ago and never came back." She exchanged a knowing glance with Summer.

"I told you about that, girls," I said with a sudden ache in my heart. "Your Mom was sick. I know it's hard for you to understand."

"She died. We know," Summer said. "It's why you were so mopey for so long. We miss her, too."

"I didn't realize —" I said.

"Of course not," Dejah said. "We couldn't say until today."

"This is all terribly tragic," said Bellzy the worblatt, not sounding at all sympathetic, "so why don't you just move along before Bub and I decide to have venison and rabbit stew for lunch?"

"Oh, deer," said Dejah.

"That's a terribly rude thing to say," said Seth the Dragon. "I think you should apologize to these new guests."

"Funny thing coming from you after what you did to Clancy," Bub said in an accusatory tone.

"Who's Clancy?" asked the great buck.

"Those are Clancy's ashes spread all over the field there, under the swarm of lake flies," Bellzy said. "Seth here committed the only real act of violence in these first 10 chapters."

"The guy was threatening my friend Grenn, here," Seth said, defensively, indicating his tiny elfin friend.

"Clancy was just coming to visit and you snuffed him!" Bub said.

"He showed up right after the Evil One rang the Chime of Doom, what was I supposed to think?" said Seth.

"We seem to have stumbled across quite a complicated incident," the doe said.

"You don't know the half of it," I agreed.

"And neither do you," said yet another new voice, this time from above.

Summer barked — in alarm or fright or surprise, it's hard to say. And the three rabbits scampered back into the woods, definitely alarmed and frightened and surprised.

It was the eagle again, and he had company.

Chapter 11
Return of the Eagle(s)

It was a convocation of eagles to be exact — the eagle we met a few minutes earlier had returned with a dozen or more friends, and they all perched along the peak of our rooftop.

"I ain't scared of you," said Bellzy the worblatt.

"Yes, you are," said the imperious eagle who had visited a few minutes ago and now was back with a few of his close friends. From the look in the big monster's eyes, the eagle was right.

"Say what you've come to say," said the great buck.

"This is interesting," murmured Dejah, who had found her way to my side during all this discussion. "The head eagle and the big horse with the antlers are both acting like they're used to being in charge."

"You're right, that's kind of funny," I said.

"It's extremely funny," Dejah said. "Everyone should know that Summer and I are in charge." I let that remark hang in the air. Being unaccustomed to my retrievers talking, I couldn't tell if she was serious or deadpan-joking.

"The events of this morning suggest fulfillment of a great prophecy in our eagle culture," said the lead eagle.

"Let me guess," said Grenn the elfin one, his eyes rolling.

"Please don't interrupt," the eagle said, unaccustomed to being interrupted. "The prophecy says, 'In the time of magic there will come a day when the dimensions merge and tongues are unlocked to a human. Be on watch —'"

"'Be on watch against the Evil One on that day, lest it consume all in its path.' Yeah, yeah. tell me something we don't know," Grenn said.

"I guess the prophecy wasn't from elf culture OR dragon culture," Seth the Dragon admitted.

"Doesn't matter," Grenn said. "What are we going to do about it?"

"We came because we heard a loud voice that seemed to be coming from everywhere at once," he eagle said. "Was that the Evil One?"

"I was just going to ask our tall companions here," said the great buck, indicating Bellzy and Bub, the worblatts, who looked uncomfortable.

"Well, to be perfectly honest —" said Bub.

"Yeah, of course it was the Evil One," Bellzy interrupted. "Who else would want to destroy everything in his path?"

If Dejah had eyebrows, they would have lifted, but she remained silent.

"Well, then, what are we going to do about this?" asked the doe, who was a little distracted because the fawns had started to prance around each other.

"Why would we discuss strategy with two of the Evil One's allies standing in that field listening?" The eagle had a point.

"Are the dimensions really merging?" Summer asked suddenly.

"What?" said several beings at once.

"Well, there's that inter-dimensional portal thing, and the worblatts and the really big guy came through, but is that the same thing as the dimensions merging?" Summer said. "If whole dimensions were banging together, wouldn't there be a little more — what's the word? — chaos going on?"

"We got a human who can suddenly understand what we're talking about, and a small crowd of us getting more crowded by the minute," Grenn said. "Isn't that chaotic enough for ya?"

"My little sister has a point," Dejah said. "This is the time of magic — it's October, after all — and it's a really weird day, but is it really THAT day?"

"Oh, come on, guys," said Bellzy. "I'm telling you, it's that day. Why else would the boss be here?"

"But he hesitated," Seth said. "He got all worked up when the dogs asked why he wanted to destroy everything, but then he walked off to think about it instead of just going ahead and destroying us all."

Everyone turned to look at the worblatts, who appeared to be conflicted. After a few moments of awkward silence, Bub seemed to make up his mind.

"I'm going to tell them," Bub said.

"Don't you dare!" Bellzy flared.

Chapter 12
An Accidental Revelation

"The truth is that —" Bub said.

That was all he was able to say before Bellzy tackled him.

Do you know what it's like when one 20-foot-tall worblatt tackles another 20-foot-tall worblatt and they crash to the ground? Even the great buck was lifted off the ground by the shock wave, and Seth the Dragon teetered a tad.

"Don't hurt the septic mound!" I cried.

The two worblatts wrestled on the field in front of the septic mound.

"Watch out for the willows!" I shouted. After all, the name of the property is Three Willows, and I like having three big willow trees.

Bellzy and Bub rolled away from the trees and toward —

"Don't break the fence!!!" I screamed.

"Gentlemen, gentlemen," Seth said, stepping over the backyard fence and gently laying a clawed paw on the shoulder of the worblatt on top, who happened to be Bellzy at that moment.

"What the —?!" cried Bellzy, who swung an arm up and back and accidentally smacked the dragon in the snout.

"All right, THAT'S ENOUGH!" Now Seth was rather irritated. Even the two battling worblatts had to stop battling at the menacing sound of an irritated dragon's voice.

"Fine, I won't tell them the truth," Bub said as he sat on the ground and Bellzy eased himself back up to his full height.

"Too late," Dejah said, her tail wagging uncertainly. "Now you've got us curious."

"Yes," said the imperious bald eagle on the room, and his fellow eagles ruffled their wings in tacit agreement. "Tell us what you're hiding about the Evil One."

"He's not —" Bub began, but he was silenced by a backhand across the face. "Hey! That hurt, Bellzy."

"It was supposed to hurt," said his colleague. "It was also supposed to get you to. shut. up!"

"That's kind of rude," said Summer.

"I don't care!" Bellzy said. "You're not supposed to know that's not really the Evil One!"

The big worblatt stopped suddenly with a shocked look on his face, as if disbelieving he had just said what he just said.

The silence was not broken until Grenn, the elfin being, broke into a wide grin and said, "Oops."

Dejah also seemed to be smiling, and she said, "Well, this is an interesting turn of events."

The eagles looked at each other in something akin to confusion.

"So this is NOT the day foretold in the great prophecy?" one of the big birds said.

"No, no, it is!" Bub said, but his body language reminded me of Frank Morgan trying to get Dorothy to pay no attention to the man behind the curtain.

"This is the day when the dimensions merge and the Evil One comes to destroy everything! This is it! Run, everyone, run!"

"Give it up, Bub," said Bellzy. "I just blew it."

"Something tells me we still need to be on guard," said Seth the Dragon.

"Agreed," said the arrogant eagle. "This is still an unusual day even for the time of magic."

"What's going on here, boys?" the great buck asked the worblatts.

"You'll find out soon enough," said Bellzy defiantly but a little hopelessly, and turning to Bub, he added, "He's going to kill us when he finds out."

"FINDS OUT WHAT?" asked a voice that seemed to come from everywhere at once.

Chapter 13
Return of Not the Evil One

The creature formerly known as the Evil One emerged from the woods and strode back into the field looking down at the two 20-foot-tall worblatts.

"I'M GOING TO KILL YOU WHEN I FIND OUT … WHAT?" The Thing said.

Bellzy and Bub looked at each other, seemed to be silently arguing which one had to say it, and then looked up at their boss.

"Please, sir," Bub said, and he almost seemed to curtsy. "We accidentally told them that you aren't the Evil One."

Because The Thing was not a dragon, he could not emit smoke from his nostrils, but even so, he seemed to smolder for a few, very comfortable seconds.

At last, he said as quietly as a being larger than a worblatt could, "YOU HAD ONE JOB."

"Well, yes," Bellzy admitted, "but in Bub's defense, I was actually the one who let it slip."

"Huh," Grenn said. "Honor among worblatts. Who woulda thunk."

"SILENCE!" screamed The Thing as if he was a parody of a bad B-movie villain, that is to say, almost a parody of a parody.

And so we were all silent for another beat or two, or three.

"Are you going to kill us?" Bub asked, almost hopefully. "Or are you going to hurt us for a very long time, and then kill us?"

"I'M THINKING! I'M THINKING!" The Thing screamed.

"I must say, you are a very indecisive villain," Dejah said. "First you went away to take time to decide if you're going destroy everything, now you're taking time to decide how to punish your worblatts."

"HOW DARE YOU? DON'T YOU KNOW WHO I AM?"

"Now you sound like the eagle," Summer said from the deck.

"And no, if you're not the Evil One, we *don't* know who you are," the eagle said from the roof.

"Fellas, I don't know if we want to irritate him any more than we have already," said Grenn the elfin one.

"SILENCE!" screamed The Thing.

"Now you're just repeating yourself," said Seth the Dragon.

At that, the whatever-it-was that had been mistaken for the Evil One reared up, which made Seth rear up on his hind legs the way he had just before he turned Clancy the worblatt into ash.

They hung in time like that for what felt like an eternity, and smoke began to creep from the dragon's nose and mouth.

Then, and I swear this is true, Seth said, "Go ahead. Make my day."

They kept hanging in time for what felt like an eternity, and then, perhaps proving beyond a shadow of a doubt that The Thing was indeed a parody of a bad B-movie villain, he began to laugh a slow laugh. It was an evil laugh, the kind of laugh that a bad B-movie villain laughs when his bluff has been called but he's not quite ready to back down.

"VERY WELL," said The Thing, "HOLD YOUR ATOMIC BREATH, GODZILLA."

"I know that was intended as an insult," Seth said, "but thank you for the compliment."

"ALL RIGHT!" The Thing snapped. "I'M NOT THE EVIL ONE, SO I CAN'T CONSUME ALL IN MY PATH."

"Thank goodness," said the doe, whose fawns were cowering behind her and the great buck.

"BUT THAT DOESN'T MEAN YOU'RE ALL SAFE," the enormous being continued. "AND IT DOESN'T MEAN TODAY IS NOT THE DAY OF THE EVIL ONE."

"Uh oh," Grenn said.

"IT ONLY MEANS HE'S NOT HERE YET," said The Thing.

I began to wonder how I would write how the Evil One might talk. All-caps plus boldface? Not that that was my biggest worry.

"AS FOR YOU TWO," the creature said, turning to Bellzy and Bub, who were trying to cower behind each other.

What was about to happen next had to wait, because of what did happen next.

Chapter 14
Halftime Show

The phone rang.

It was work.

"I can't let this go to voicemail, would you folks mind if —" I asked the assembled multitude.

Grenn the elf looked amused. Seth the Dragon looked confused. The eagles looked irritated. Summer and Dejah looked around as if they were worried about how the others might react. As for the two worblatts and their enormous boss, they looked frightened and angry, respectively, but that didn't seem to have anything to do with me.

I hit the green button on my phone.

"Hey," I said.

"Say, Warren, how's that city council story you promised coming?"

I closed my eyes in embarrassment. "I said I was going to have that for you last night, didn't I?"

There was a long, familiar silence.

"You forgot to do it," said the long-suffering voice on the other end.

"I keep telling you I need to retire," I said, only half joking.

"OK, you think you can have it later today, at least?"

"Yeah, I hope so," I said. "I'm kind of in the middle of something here."

"It better be the end of the world as we know it," my colleague said.

"Ha ha. Yeah, it's something like that. Thanks for understanding."

"Did I say I understand?"

"No, but you always cut me slack, and I appreciate it more than you know."

"Right. I'll be looking for that story."

"It's coming," I said. "Bye."

I hit the red button on my phone.

The sun was flitting in and out among the clouds, and the wind chimes were making a melodic tuneless tune in the light breeze. Out in the field the cloud of lake flies undulated over the tall grass and remains of summer wildflowers — goldenrod, white clover, compass plants, coneflowers and Black-eyed Susans.

"Did you really have to take that call?" I was surprised at how very irritated the eagle was, of all things.

"It was work, I can't ignore when work calls," I said.

"Remember the part where there's a prophecy about how the Evil One will come to consume everything in his path on a certain day, and all of the signs are saying today is that day?" said Grenn the elfin being.

"Look, the one thing I know about prophecies is no one knows the day or the hour," I said. "On the other hand, I know exactly the day and the hour that I have to get that city council story done. Do you mind?"

"Blasphemy!" screeched one of the eagles.

"Oh dear," said Dejah.

"So," said Seth the Dragon, turning to the giant who was not the Evil One after all, "if you're not the

Evil One after all, who are you, and what is this all about?"

Not the Evil One sneered down at all of us.

"WOULDN'T YOU LIKE TO KNOW?"

"Of course we would like to know," Summer said in all sincerity.

"TOO BAD."

And with that, the giant snapped his fingers. Bellzy and Bub the worblatts screamed, there was a bright light and a roaring sound, and the three huge beings disappeared.

For a moment only the wind chimes made any sound.

"What just happened?" asked the great buck.

"Mama, I'm scared," said one of the fawns.

"Me too," said the other fawn.

"It's going to be all right, kids," said the doe, but then looked at her mate for reassurance. "Isn't it?"

Grenn the elf exchanged a look with Seth the Dragon.

"I honestly don't know," said the elf.

Chapter 15
Taking Stock

"OK," Dejah said then. "Let's just assume that the Evil One is coming, and he has at least a couple of worblatts and that big whoever-he-is guy working for him. What do we do?"

"I'm going to go inside and hide," Summer said.

"Right. Good dog," Dejah told her little sister. "As for the rest of us, who do we have to defend the universe? My dear Daddy, who's a pacifist but at least he feeds us twice a day, an elfin being of some kind —
"

"I would tell you the name of our kind, but you couldn't pronounce it," Grenn said with a grim smile.

"Hey! Like Spock," Dejah said, and seeing the look on my face, added, "I told you. I watch *Star Trek* with you. Can you watch it more often, please?"

"I'll keep that in mind," I promised.

"All right, so in order of appearance — not counting the worblatt foot — and darn it, Daddy, pick up the yard when this is over! — we have Grenn, the eagles, Seth the Dragon, and the great buck and his family," Dejah said, and calling to the white-tailed deer family, asked, "What are your names anyway?"

"Names? We have no names," said the buck. "We know who we are."

"Holy cow, an obscure *Fantastic Four* reference," Grenn said.

"You know the Fantastic Four?" I gasped. "That's impossible, man!"

"Yes, it is," the elf said with an appreciative smile. "Good one."

"What was that all about?" Seth asked.

"If you know, you know," said Grenn. "Moving on, I could probably get a few of my friends together to handle this thing."

"And the deer world is with you," said the doe.

"And as you can see, I have already mustered my finest warriors," the eagle said, indicating the convocation of eagles perched along my rooftop.

"You figure we're going into battle, then," I said uneasily.

"What else does one do when our world is threatened with extinction?" asked the eagle. "We defend our homes!"

"We don't even know if the prophecy is real —" I began.

"Blasphemy!" one of the eagles screeched. It was the same eagle who had screeched that word, before. Perhaps it was the only English word he knew.

"— and even if it is, we don't know if today is the day it predicted!" I finished.

"What day is that?" asked Summer, whose short-term memory is almost as bad as mine.

The elf, the dragon and the head eagle grew serious and chanted in unison, ""In the time of magic there will come a day when the dimensions merge and tongues are unlocked to a human. Be on watch against the Evil One on that day, lest it consume all in its path."

"You really think this is all about that?" asked the buck.

Grenn looked at the four deer with a frustrated expression, which then softened. "Oh, that's right. You're new here. Yes, we're thinking this might be the day of the great prophecy, especially since —" indicating yours truly — "he usually can't understand a word any of us says."

"Oh — 'tongues are unlocked to a human' — I see," said the doe.

"So we're on watch against the Evil One, to keep it from consuming everything in its path," said the dragon.

"What do we do now?" asked one of the fawns.

"We wait," the lead eagle said.

I put an affectation in my voice and added, "And wait. And wait. And wait. And wait. And wait."

"That reminds me," Summer said. "Can we watch *Casablanca* again when this is over?"

"I wouldn't have taken you for an old movie buff," Seth said.

"I'm not. But I think Claude Rains is a hottie," said Summer.

The eagle looked perplexed. "Clawed rains? How do you claw rain?"

As if on cue — I've been saying that a lot, haven't I? — a tremendous lightning bolt struck in the middle of the field, making us all jump, and in the smoking place where the lightning had struck, something began to emerge.

Chapter 16
That Which Emerges

What appeared out of the cloud of smoke was — a man. Just a plain man in jeans and a T-shirt. And he was smiling kind of a simpering smile that said hey, here I am, I'm pretty cool, who the hell are you?

"Hey folks," he said when he sauntered close enough to carry on a normal conversation. "What dimension is this?"

"This is reality, Greg," said Dejah, earning a surprised look from me that she knew another ancient pop culture reference. "What? Do you realize how many times you've watched E.T.?"

"Yes, but the question is, *which* reality?" the man said. "And how did you know my name is Greg?"

"Lucky guess," said my ancient English cream golden retriever, rolling her eyes.

"Wait," Greg said. "I see a convocation of eagles, some white-tailed deer, a dragon, and a —" he then said a word that had three syllables but involved contorting his mouth, throat and tongue in ways that human mouths, throats and tongues can't actually do.

Grenn's eyes widened in surprise. "How did you pronounce my people's name?"

"Piece of cake in my reality," said the gentleman known as Greg. "So I'm going to guess this is dimension 5-D."

"It kind of feels like dimension number 1 to me," said Seth the Dragon.

"Oh, everyone believes that," Greg said, "but that's my dimension. Trust me, you folks are 5-D."

"Be that as it may," said the eagle from his perch above it all, "what are you doing here?"

"Taking advantage of the situation, of course," said the newcomer. "You *have* noticed, I presume, that I, who am human, am able to understand and communicate with you?"

"That goes without saying," said Dejah, which for some reason made Greg laugh out loud.

"Exactly," he said.

"Who exactly did you say you are?" asked Grenn the elf, who seemed more wary than the rest of us, and believe me, we were pretty wary ourselves.

"Why, I just told you, I'm Greg, from dimension #1."

"Actually, the old dog called you Greg, and you went along with it," Grenn said. "You're not who you want us to believe you are. No human from any dimension can pronounce the name of my race."

The newcomer grinned a wide grin — actually it was a wider grin than any human can muster. His face became rubbery and more elongated, and his skin began to turn a greenish hue.

"I probably shouldn't have shown off like that," he said. "I would have fooled you for more than a few seconds if I wasn't such a darn show-off. Oh well."

He opened his arms wide, and a bright light appeared above the house. The eagles flew away and began to circle the land as the light grew brighter and brighter.

"Daddy?" On the deck, Summer stepped to the top of the stairs. "I don't feel so good. I don't — I don't know what's happening."

She staggered a little, and I took the stairs two steps at a time. "You're all right?"

The light grew brighter and brighter, and my little girl stumbled into my arms and said, "I don't want to go! I don't want to go! Daddy, please."

The sudden flash was so bright it hurt our eyes, and then it was gone.

And so was Summer. My arms were empty. My dog was gone.

"Seth?" This was the elfin voice of Grenn, which turned into a shout. "SETH!"

The dragon was gone, too.

"What have you done?" This was my voice, and it was Grenn's voice, and it was the eagle's voice, and it was the mighty buck's voice. We turned at once and said it simultaneously to the being called Greg.

"Well, the truth is —" the newcomer said, and he paused as if deciding whether to finish the sentence, and then did: "I am the Evil One."

Chapter 17
Stuff Gets Real

No one spoke for quite a few seconds. And then Dejah began to growl.

I have never heard such a sound from the throat of a golden retriever. They are gentle, happy animals. This was neither gentle nor happy. My 11-year-old dog was growling like a K-9 officer who had just been given permission to rip a perp to shreds.

Gone was the gentle English cream golden retriever that had yipped at the door hoping to get a treat when she came in the house. Gone, too, was the genteel canine who had been politely carrying on conversations with me, the elf, the dragon and the other visitors on this "day of magic." She wasn't even using words, just making the guttural noises that an animal makes moments before it launches an attack.

And launch she did. Moving at a speed that belied her status as an elderly dog, Dejah bolted toward the fence as if to leap over it and dismember the creature in T-shirt and jeans who had just disappeared her little sister and a big dragon.

I was right behind her. Screaming, "What did you to my dog?!" I sprinted toward him with a roiling hatred in my soul that made me fear for the guy when I got my hands on him — if Dejah didn't reach him with her fangs and claws first.

In the corner of my eye, I saw Grenn the elfin being raise his left hand, palm up like a Marvel superhero sorcerer about to cast a spell. All of a sudden I couldn't move, and Dejah suddenly stopped and writhed like a rabid animal at the end of her leash.

"Let me go!" she barked. "I'm going to kill him!!"

"I don't think you want to try that," Grenn said.

"No," said the man who had just identified himself as the Evil One, smirking. "It would not end well for you."

At that, Grenn made a sweeping motion with his right hand, and the smirking man's head snapped sideways and back. He was lifted off the ground and flattened as if the elf had planted a right hook on him from 25 feet away.

Greg, or whatever his real name was, rubbed his chin and smiled as he picked himself off the ground and faced us.

"I will forgive you that," he said. "You are grieving and not thinking straight."

"What have you done to my dog?" I repeated.

"And my friend Seth," repeated the elf.

"Isn't it obvious?" said the creature, who now had green skin and an elongated face, similar to a character I cannot describe further without risking a copyright violation on *Fantastic Four* #11. "They're not here anymore."

"Where are they?" asked the eagle leader from the sky, where he continued to circle with his feathered colleagues.

"Gone, of course," the creature said. The eagle responded by diving toward the beast, pulling up with his claws extended, and taking a piece of green flesh off the arm he had raised defensively. Seven of the other eagles swooped down and did a bit of scratching of their own.

There was another blinding flash, and suddenly the eagles were 100 feet in the air. The great buck lowered his great rack of antlers and began to charge.

"Stop right there or you're next!" The creature cried. The deer decided to pull up. "You're all fools! Why are you resisting? The whole point of this day is for the Evil One to consume all in its path."

"Which is why we're on guard," said the buck. "You do know the prophecy, don't you?"

"Of course I do," said the green thing, who was bleeding from dozens of eagle scratches. The great birds circled, preparing for another swoop.

"Liar!" screamed Grenn the elf, using his Big Voice. "But that's who the Evil One is, the Prince of Liars."

"All right, that's ENOUGH!" the green thing shouted and raised both hands to the sky.

This flash was the most blinding of all.

Chapter 18
Hope and Jeopardy

And then the bad guy was gone.

I stood at the fence with Dejah panting by my side. Grenn, the elfin being, stood at the edge of the woods behind me. The great buck, his mate and their two fawns stepped cautiously off the septic mound and onto the field. The eagles circled and lined up in a row along the top of the mound, which rises 10-12 feet at the edge of the field.

"I don't get it," Grenn said. "He zapped the strongest of us, and the meekest. I get why the dragon, but why the goofy dog?"

At the word "meekest," tears had sprung to my eyes. Summer was a crazy animal who loved to torment and wrestle with her older sister, but one day when I picked them up after doggie day care, the lady at the desk said, "Summer is such a kind dog," and the word fit perfectly. Rambunctious and silly, yes, but above all, Summer was kind. Why would that monster zap her?

And the word "zap" also struck me.

"You said he zapped them," I said. "You don't think he killed them?"

Dejah's ears perked up.

"No, or at least I don't think so," Grenn said. "Did you see what happened when he zapped the eagles? He just, like, teleported them a lot higher. I think he sent Seth and your dog somewhere, maybe even somewhere near here."

Dejah's tail began to wag.

"So he didn't vaporize them with a phaser, he beamed them away?" Dejah said. "That is most pleasant news."

"I agree," I said. "But where could they be? Summer is such a gentle soul, and she has to be frightened."

"That's probably the answer to 'why' — Seth obviously had the best chance of frying the little creep, but evil ones can't stand being in the presence of kind and gentle souls,' said the elf.

"'Evil ones,'" the buck caught the nuance. "You don't think that he is THE Evil One, just an evil being of a lesser sort?"

"Makes more sense," Grenn said. "The Evil One doesn't hesitate, it just swoops in and destroys everything in its path. The tall guy with his worblatt pals and the green guy did some damage, but nothing on the scale that the prophecy talks about."

"So who are they?" asked Dejah. "And why are they bothering us?"

"Minions," guessed the doe. "And it's a distraction."

"You mean if the Evil One is really coming, it's not here or now?" the buck asked, and his mate nodded.

"If that's true —" the lead eagle began, but he wasn't able to complete the sentence.

Another blinding flash flashed, and the impossible green guy was back, holding some kind of weapon. It looked like something out of a Jack Kirby comic book, way too large for his hand and full of mechanical protuberances but definitely some sort of outsized gun.

"Everybody duck!" Grenn shouted.

Crackling energy crackled, and the gun emitted a sizzling beam of something bright and electrical that you wouldn't want to get hit by. It missed me but left a charred hole in the yard behind me.

The deer disappeared into the woods. Dejah and I dashed across the yard and up onto the deck, I yanked the patio door open and we dove into the house. Grenn waved his hand as the green creature aimed at the eagles, and some sort of magic shield deflected a shot that would have blasted the eagle leader.

Dejah and I stood by the window and watched in horror as the green guy leveled his weapon directly at the house.

"FOOOOOM!"

Chapter 19
Down the Road

A few minutes earlier …

Summer opened her eyes and saw that she was on a sandy beach next to a great expanse of water. The sand had washed away some, and there were deposits of thousands and thousands of tiny mussel shells. It had to be a large lake or perhaps a bay, because she could see the other side, miles away.

On the beach next to her, Seth the Dragon looked down with concern.

"You're awake," said the giant scaled creature. "I think you fainted or something."

The 3-year-old golden retriever looked into the dragon's eyes and then across the water.

"Is this heaven?" she asked.

"Nah," Seth said. "It's called Red River Park, on the shore of Green Bay. It's a couple miles from where you live."

"I don't understand," said Summer. "How did we get here? And how did we survive that big bright light?"

"It wasn't a weapon, at least not a weapon that kills people," the dragon said. "It just moves you. It's a teleporter."

"I see why he would want to get rid of you," said the little golden retriever. "But why did he teleprompt me?"

"Teleport. Evil doesn't work very well in the face of sweetness or cuteness," Seth said. "And you're one of the sweetest, cutest things I ever did see."

"Oh, stop."

"It's true!"

Summer walked to the edge of the beach and stared at the other side of the bay. "I've never seen so much water. It's amazing."

"Your daddy never brought you down here?"

"No," Summer said. "I remember Mom used to say, 'We should take the dogs to the water,' but I didn't realize she was talking about THIS. It's wonderful."

The big puppy stepped into the water and began to prance.

"Wheeeee!" she said, because it was the Time of Magic when dogs could talk. Most days, she probably would be barking and yipping with delight.

"Why wouldn't he ever take you to such a nice place?" Seth asked.

And as if in response —

"HEY!" a sudden voice barked. "Whose DOG is this?"

The dragon stepped back, and Summer looked up as a big, beefy man strode across the beach in her direction.

"No pets in the park!! It's on the entrance sign. Can't somebody read? I'm gonna ask again: WHOSE —"

At that point the big man's eyes came to rest on the dragon.

"The dog's with me," Seth said in his voice that would sound menacing if he said "Peace be with you."

To add to the effect, he blew a little smoke out of his nostrils. "You wanna make something of it, Bubba?"

The big, beefy man screamed at several octaves higher than his normal voice and sprinted away.

Suddenly there came the sound of energy bolts crackling from some distance away. The dragon and the dog both looked in that direction.

"That's coming from your house," Seth said. "Come on!"

The dragon picked Summer up by the collar and leaped into the sky. At once they could see the bright light from the green creature's giant gun up the road.

As you've probably seen from the CGI recreations made for various movies and TV shows, dragons look like big, lumbering creatures but they are swift as lightning. They covered the short miles from the park to the house in a matter of seconds.

Seth landed behind the green alien and set Summer gently on the ground.

The evil thing leveled his enormous gun directly at the house. Seth the Dragon reared back and belched a mighty blast of flame directly at the green assailant.

"FOOOOOM!"

And just like that, there was a black smoldering hole where the green guy had been. The giant gun clattered to the ground, sputtered a few sputters, and went silent.

Chapter 20
Reunion and Omen

"Summer!" I shouted. "It's Summer!"

"Little sister!!" Dejah barked.

We ran to the patio door to slide it open, and Summer dashed up the stairs. The two dogs ran around the living room chasing each other, and then Dejah picked up the rubber circle and Summer grabbed the other side and they started a tug of war, growling with delight. After a few seconds of that, they dropped the circle and started running around the room again.

"Take it outside!" I laughed. The patio door was still open and they swept out and down the stairs again, running around the yard at each other until Dejah pulled up like an old dog that suddenly remembered she was an old dog.

"OK, OK," the old dog said. "Where have you been? What happened to you?"

"He zapped us down to Red River Park," Seth said. "Why have you never taken Summer there?!"

"No pets allowed," I said.

"Right, we heard," said the dragon. "And you always follow the rules, do ya?"

"Um —" I said, then decided to change the subject. "I think you saved my house, Seth! Thank you."

"That was a very timely appearance," said the buck.

"We were just about to strike ourselves," called the eagle, "but I must admit dragon's breath is probably more effective."

"Shucks, folks, I'm speechless," said the embarrassed dragon.

We stared at each other, and the dogs sniffed each other's noses, and it was as quiet as it had been all day.

"OK girls, in the house," I said, standing at the patio door as they scampered back up the stairs.

I was surprised to see Grenn the elfin being follow them in.

"How do you get it so warm in here without a fire?" he asked.

"Sure, come on in," I said. "Nothing miraculous, it's just the furnace."

"That's that technology stuff I've heard about, I guess," Grenn said. "Nothing that nature and magic can't do better, I would bet."

"Do you have anything like this out in the woods?" I asked, turning on the widescreen TV. A meteorologist was pointing out the usual stuff on a big weather map filled with numbers and highs and lows.

"That is actually pretty impressive," Grenn said, hopping into my TV-watching easy chair and starting at the screen.

I was kind of alarmed when the head eagle landed on the deck and hopped through the patio door. He followed Grenn's stare and saw the meteorologist doing her thing, and looked around the back of the flat screen.

"How did she get in there?" the big bird asked. "Is this magic?"

The dragon poked his nose through the patio door but pulled it out almost immediately.

"No, that's not gonna work," Seth said. The white-tailed deer stayed out on the mound talking with the eagle's friends.

"So, is that it?" I asked. "Have we foiled the great prophecy?"

"We haven't even confirmed that this is 'that' day," the eagle admitted. "And the prophecy spoke of the Evil One 'consuming all in its path,' which is not exactly what either of our two Evil Ones were doing."

"Wait a minute," Grenn said. "How do you turn the volume up on this thing?"

"What? Oh!" I said, grabbing the TV remote and pumping the volume button a few times.

"— still recovering in hurricane-devastated Florida and North Carolina," the meteorologist said. "They were two of the worst storms in recent history, consuming everything in their paths. And this new storm is like nothing I've ever seen before."

"Oh my stars," Dejah said.

"What is it?" asked Summer.

"Look at her weather map," her big sister said.

"As you can see here, the hurricane made an unusual northwestern turn in Georgia instead of following the coast," said the meteorologist. "This horrific storm appears to be heading straight for the Great Lakes."

"That's us," the eagle said.

"On its current trajectory the center of the storm will make an unprecedented strike on Northeast Wisconsin, of all things, on Halloween morning," the meteorologist said, arching an eyebrow.

Chapter 21
First sting

The two dogs, the elfin being, the eagle and I looked at each other around the TV set.

"The hurricane is the Evil One," Grenn said.

"Or the Evil One caused the hurricane," said the eagle.

"Does it really matter which?" said Dejah.

"Why is it so quiet in there?" Seth the Dragon called from outside the patio door.

The eagle hopped back outside and stretched his wings. The rest of us joined him.

"It seems we have a problem," Grenn said.

"While we've been worried about those two fake Evil Ones consuming everything in their path, there have been a couple of hurricanes that consumed everything in their paths," I said.

"They weren't fake," said the great buck. "They were evil, they just weren't THE Evil One." There were nods all around.

"And the next hurricane is coming this way," I said.

"You don't get hurricanes up this way," said Seth the Dragon.

"That's how we know it's the Evil One," the little elf guy said. "It's impossible."

"Mama, are you going to protect us from the Evil One?" asked one of the fawns.

"Aren't you tired of crying 'wolf' about this?" asked the doe, turning to our small assembly. "Isn't it more likely this is another fake?"

"They're predicting that the hurricane will reach here on Halloween morning," the eagle said, as if that settled the question. "That's the time during the Time of Magic that the magic is strongest."

There was a profound silence at this.

"I know a few guys," Grenn said. "And all you need is a few [unpronounceable]s to kick some evil magic butt."

"We're going to need more eagles," the lead eagle said, looking at his convocation of a dozen or so.

"I may be the greatest buck in these woods," said the great buck, "but there are plenty of woods and forests between here and there."

"And I'm certainly not the only dragon in the world," said Seth the Dragon.

"I have a question," said Summer, my gentle golden retriever, from the place by my side that she hadn't left since we stepped back outside. "Why is it coming here?"

"That's actually a very good question," said Dejah, her elderly sister. "Why would all the evil be focused in this place?"

As if on cue … (What, *again*?)

A spark appeared over the field in front of the mound. Slowly it grew into a rounded square, first about the size of a television screen, and then the size of an SUV, and then the size of a semi truck.

"Deer, take the kids back into the woods," the great buck said to his mate. She gave him a little glare that might have been saying, "Why is that MY job?" but did turn back and herded the two fawns away.

The inter-dimensional portal — because by now we all knew that's what it was — continued to grow until it was big enough for three worblatts to step through. And step they did.

It was Bellzy, and Bub, and another worblatt I didn't recognize, but they were definitely all worblatts, about 20 feet tall, limbs like tree limbs, and faces like the trees in *The Wizard of Oz* except on their heads instead of their torsos.

"Wait, aren't you —" began Seth the Dragon.

"— the guy you blasted into ashes?" asked the third worblatt. "Yeah, that's me, punk."

"You can't keep a good worblatt down, huh, Clancy?" said Bub.

"Got that right," said the third worblatt, who looked as grumpy as if Dorothy had been stealing his apples.

The three of them stepped back into stances that suggested they were preparing to dive into battle.

"Are you ready to rumble?" asked Bellzy. "Because we are."

Chapter 22
All lights out

Grenn put his thumb and forefinger into his mouth and emitted a sharp whistle that seemed to have a melody.

All of a sudden, as if from out of nowhere, the little elf was joined by two or three dozen other elfin beings, some of them armed with what looked like bows and arrows, a few of them in blue robes decorated with stars and sparkles as if they were sorcerer's apprentices, and most of them dressed in animal skins like Grenn himself.

The head eagle emitted a loud cry, and within moments the convocation of a dozen or so eagles doubled in size, and I could see more eagles approaching in the sky.

The great buck didn't say a thing that I could hear, but a half-dozen huge bucks walked out of the woods and joined their colleague standing on the mound.

Seth the Dragon leaned his head back and set a pillar of flame shooting high into the sky, and in a blink of an eye there were four more dragons hovering in positions surrounding the three worblatts.

Summer, noticing that I had left the patio door open, lunged into the house. Dejah stood next to me but began to inch toward the door herself.

"I don't suppose you folks could take this a little farther away from my house?" I asked plaintively.

The three worblatts seemed to falter and reconsider whether they were ready to rumble.

"Come on, guys," Clancy said. "Shall we go down swinging?"

"No, this is good," Bellzy said. "Now we know who they can muster, how many and how fast."

They stepped back into the inter-dimensional portal, which zipped up and vanished as if it had never been there.

"Huh. That was easy," said one of the elves.

"Almost — TOO easy," said Grenn. "We played our hand, and they sneered at our steenkin' hand."

"What are you talking about?" Seth said. "They took one look at all of us and stepped back into whatever dimension they came from."

"— while making comments about our ability to rally the troops," said Grenn. "I don't know. I have a bad feeling about this."

"Next thing you know, the green guy will be coming back to torment you," someone said.

"I don't think so," the big dragon said. "I torched him pretty good."

"Um, Seth?" Dejah said.

"Yeah, doggie, what's up?" said Seth the Dragon.

"It's the green guy."

Everyone was looking at the newcomer with the elongated head, T-shirt and jeans leaning up against the fence.

"What? Impossible!"

The little green monster grinned an enormous grin and waved his hand in greeting. There came an enormously bright flash.

Chapter 24
The [unpronounceables]

And just as suddenly as he had appeared, the green guy vanished.

"What in heaven's name was that all about?" Dejah asked.

"I thought I killed him," said Seth the Dragon. "And Clancy the worblatt."

"You're losing your touch, Seth," one of the other dragons said.

"That's OK, I don't like killing folks," Seth said. "I'd rather hurt him real bad."

"Evil beings don't die so easily anyway," said the leader of the eagles. "They wanted to taunt us and make us doubt our power and ability."

"Now we know when they're coming," said Grenn the elfin being. "Hurricane force on Halloween morning, and this seems to be the epicenter."

"I still don't understand why it's all happening here," I said. "There's nothing special or especially magical about this place."

"Speak for yourself," said Summer.

I saw the faraway look in my younger dog's eyes and realized she was right. My wife and I called this little plot of land Serenity Valley, and the enormous willow trees — which were sticks in the ground when we planted them — led me to dub the estate Three Willows after I lost her. I have spent a dozen years writing about how special and magical this place is, a place that the most evil of evils would have to hate and possibly destroy.

I looked at Grenn, my new little friend from the race of elfin beings whose name I could not pronounce.

"And who are you anyway, Grenn?" I asked. "You said you were here before we built the house."

"And for a thousand generations before that," said the [unpronounceable]. "Minding our own business until you people started crowding us out."

"I asked you before, why didn't you let us know you were here? Maybe we could have worked something out," I said.

"We didn't think that was who you are," Grenn said. "Now that I've gotten to know you a little, maybe you're not so bad."

One of the other [unpronounceables], one with a sorcerer's robe, came up next to Grenn with an urgent look on his face.

"If the Evil One is bringing a hurricane here, we need to start planning," the mystic one said. "We have spells to cast, potions to conjure. We have to stop wasting time."

"But we want to help," Dejah said. The little person in the robe rolled his eyes.

"We don't need your help."

"Actually, Blurg, the dogs have been somewhat useful so far," Grenn said.

"Ri-ight," said the one named Blurg. "All they ever do is chase squirrels and foul the yard."

"I don't mean to intrude," said Seth the Dragon in a low purr — the problem with a dragon purring is even that sounds menacing. "You're talking about friends of mine."

"Aww, thanks," Summer said. "You're our friend, too — I think. Seth *is* our friend, isn't he, Dejah?"

"Of course he is, don't be silly," said Dejah.

"You little guys are terrific with the magic stuff," said the dragon, "but I think beating this thing might take all of us working together."

"I'm with you there," Grenn said, earning a wide-eyed "Harrumph" from Blurg. "Oh, go round up the others and start preparing some spells and such. I'll be with you in a few minutes."

Blurg stalked off as if he had been dismissed, which of course he had been.

"To answer your question, we are everywhere, living what you humans would call a sustainable life," Grenn said. "We return what we take from the land in ways that leave it exactly as we found it. That's why it's so easy to escape detection unless we choose for you to detect us."

"Given what I've seen today, I think there's a lot going on in these woods that have escaped detection by our civilization," I said.

One of the [unpronounceables] guffawed. "Your 'civilization' ain't exactly civilized."

"What about you?" I asked, turning to the eagle. "There seems to be an eagle warrior society of some kind going on."

"It's nice of you to ask," the eagle chief said. "Let me tell you about it."

Chapter 24
Eagles and dragons and deer, oh my

And he told us. And told us. And told us. And told us. And told us.

My first impression of the eagle had been that he was pretty full of himself. After all, his first words to me had been, basically, "Don't you know who I am?"

All I had asked was for the eagle to tell us a little bit about eagle society. There followed a lengthy exposition of eagle history, regarding how eagles have proudly defended their heritage against any and all foes through the ages. This particular eagle chief was particularly heroic, and he was happy to describe just how heroic he was.

"All well and good," Dejah said after a very long while. "What can you guys do about the Evil One and its hurricane?"

"What can we do? What can we DO?" the eagle said huffily. "Why don't you just go inside your house and have a little doggie bone, and leave the fighting to me and my valiant eagle colleagues."

"I'm thinking we need to work together, all of us," suggested Seth the Dragon.

"Have you ever seen an eagle wait patiently in the sky until he was ready to seize his prey, then swoop down and inevitably vanquish his target?" asked the chief eagle. "Now imagine dozens of eagles diving at the foe, talons at the ready to slash and destroy. It will be a glorious sight."

"Sound icky," said Summer.

"Well, yes," the eagle replied. "That's the point."

"How are you going to slash and destroy a hurricane?" asked one of the dragons. "It's just wind."

"Clearly you have never seen us in action," the eagle said indignantly.

"And clearly you didn't answer the question," the great buck said wryly.

"OK, so me and my folks will be ready with some spells and counter-spells and stuff," said Grenn the [unpronounceable]. "And the eagles have a lot of pointy things to slash the wind. What do you have, deer?"

The big buck looked a little perplexed. "I have to admit, I am not as confident as our feathered friend. I have these" — he glanced up at his great rack of antlers — "but as our giant scaly friend pointed out, we're planning to fight the wind."

"And a few worblatts," Summer said. "And that guy who was taller than the worblatts. And the little green guy with the bright teleprompter light."

"Teleport," I said, trying not to smile. "Oh, Summer, you're so cute."

"You have five of us," said Seth the Dragon. "That's four more than you need to vanquish an Evil One."

"Dragons and [unpronounceables] have magic on our side," Grenn said. "And October is The Time of Magic, and Halloween is when magic is most powerful. The hurricane may be some kind of evil magic, but we know a little something about casting magic ourselves."

"You'll both be at the height of your powers on Halloween," the buck said. "Both you and the forces of evil."

"Should I start putting plywood over my windows, stuff like that?" I asked. "I've never lived in hurricane country, it's like asking someone in Louisiana to get ready for a blizzard."

"If this hurricane has the power of the Evil One behind it, don't bother," the eagle chief said. "Your house will be utterly destroyed."

"You are one of the least cheerful people I've ever met," Dejah told the big bird.

"Silence, cur," the eagle sneered.

"What's a cur?" The old dog asked.

"It's a mongrel or an inferior dog," one of the [unpronounceables] said.

"I'll have you know I'm a purebred English cream golden retriever," Dejah said proudly.

"What's that mean?" asked one of the eagle's fellows.

"It means she's a high-class cur who will be useless in a battle."

"That's really not nice, bird," Seth said.

"This isn't helping," said the buck. "We need to be figuring out how to defend this land, not fighting among ourselves."

"Yeah," Bellzy the worblatt said, stepping through the dimensional portal and into the field once again. "You never know when the bad guys might attack."

Chapter 25
Skirmish

Bellzy stepped onto the small field in front of the septic mound. His friend Clancy, who had been incinerated and then refreshed somehow, stepped through next, checking the ground as if to make sure it was free of dog poo. Finally, Bub came through and stood with his comrades.

"Hi again, folks, remember us?" Bellzy said, looking confidently around at the assembled eagles, white-tailed deer, dragons and [unpronounceables]. "So here's how it's going to be. We're setting up camp to prepare for the coming of the Evil One."

"I thought the Evil One was that giant buffoon who shouted all the time," Dejah said. "Oh, that's right, he got mad when you admitted he wasn't really the Evil One."

"You're pretty sassy for a mutt," said Clancy, taking a step towards her. "Maybe I oughtta teach you some manners."

"Careful, Summer and Daddy were out there yesterday and I think she pooped."

"WHAT?!" Clancy shouted, losing his balance as he looked at the ground in alarm, flailing and falling over with a BOOM. For a 20-foot worblatt, the guy had a serious phobia for dog poop.

The mystic [unpronounceable] named Blurg came up next to Grenn, and I realized suddenly that I had mistaken her for a little male wizard.

"I have an idea," she said. "Cover me." Blurg made a circle with her hand, a small inter-dimensional portal appeared, and she stepped through with a half-dozen other [unpronounceables].

"I'm rather sure this gentleman does not welcome worblatts camping on his property," the great buck said to the worblatts.

"What's he going to do about it?" Bub said.

In answer, the bucks and dragons took a step forward, surrounding the three giants, and the eagles began to circle overhead.

"Oh, mommy, I'm scared," said Bellzy, using that childlike taunt that grownup villains assume when they're not scared at all.

The dimensional portal through which they had entered was still open, or else seven rotten tomatoes would not have been able to emerge from the portal and smack the three worblatts on the side of their angry-looking heads just then.

"Hey!" said Bellzy.

"What the —?" said Bub.

"EWW!" said Clancy.

Through the portal we could see Blurg and four of her companions standing in a field on the other side.

"Get them!" Bellzy shouted, and he and his two comrades dove back through the portal and began running after the little elfin beings.

As soon as they were out of sight, two other [unpronounceable] mystics stepped forward, hopped through the portal to our side, and made several elaborate gestures while chanting something I could never pronounce.

The portal closed with a rather unpleasant zipping sound.

"Sealed!" One of the mystics cried.

"What about Blurg and the others?" Summer asked with her usual trepidation.

In a few moments, another portal re-formed next to Grenn and the five other mystics leapt through. Blurg came through last, stumbling to the ground. From her sitting position she made the same gestures and incantations her colleagues had used. An enormous worblatt hand reached through the portal and the closing portal zipped around it.

"OW! OW! OW!" came a voice that sounded like Clancy's, and the hand pulled back through before the final, unpleasant zipping sound that sealed the portal.

"Is it my imagination," asked the regal eagle, "or are worblatts all clumsy oafs?"

"Great job, Blurg," Grenn said, giving her a hug that suggested — at least to me — that they might be more than just fellow warriors.

"Piece of pie," Blurg replied.

Another elfin being opened the patio door and came out onto the deck. Through the glass I could see several [unpronounceables] sitting on the floor in front of my television.

Before I could voice my thought that everyone was getting a bit too comfortable, the elf on the deck said, "I think you need to see this."

Chapter 26

The target

Dejah, Summer and I entered our living room, accompanied by a few of the creatures and critters who were small enough to get through the patio door. The TV was still tuned to the weather channel, and a bewildered meteorologist was pointing to the weather map, which showed something I had never seen on a weather map before: a kind of red arch of an arrow anchored in the southeastern United States and with the point more or less pointing to my land — or at least an area just east of the bay of Green Bay.

"This is history in the making, folks," said the weather person, who looked excited and frightened simultaneously. "The hurricane appears to have launched itself into the mesosphere, about 60 miles high, from a spot in the middle of the Gulf of Mexico. It's on a high arc and on a course that seems targeted to land on Northeast Wisconsin from above."

"The Evil One," Grenn and Blurg said simultaneously.

Blurg gave Grenn a gentle punch in the shoulder and said, "You owe me a mead."

"It's still due to make landfall — maybe we should call that skyfall — about 20 miles north of Green Bay, Wisconsin, on Halloween morning," the meteorologist said. "Some scientists are calling it a byproduct of climate change, but I have to say, I don't know what to call it. This is simply unprecedented."

"It's magic," Grenn and Blurg said simultaneously. Blurg poked Grenn in the shoulder again.

"Yeah, yeah, that makes two," Grenn grinned.

I had two conflicting feelings. I was thankful that whatever was coming our way was apparently not going to wreak havoc and destruction for 1,000 miles from the Gulf of Mexico to my home. At the same time I was horrified that I appeared to be living at Ground Zero.

"Why in the wide, wide world of sports would this magic hurricane be targeting *my house*??!!" I cried.

"What's the wide, wide, world of sports?" Blurg asked.

"Before your time, dear," Grenn said.

"*Blazing Saddles* reference," Dejah said.

"What's *Blazing Saddles*?" Summer said.

"Oh my gosh, Daddy, we haven't watched *Blazing Saddles* in more than three years!" Dejah cried.

"Summer, I owe you a laurel and hearty handshake," I told her. "But, back on topic, why is this evil hurricane coming here?"

"The Evil One works in strange and mysterious ways," said the eagle chief, and I was surprised to see him in my living room again. People were coming and going so quickly.

"It's not that mysterious," said Grenn. "Come on, everybody, let's go outside. Philbert, you keep an eye on that magic box, to monitor any other news we need to know."

"Oh, man. Why am I always on monitor duty?" asked Philbert.

"It's what you do best," said Grenn, which brought a smile to Philbert's face.

"OK, boss," he said. "Thanks."

We gathered in front of the septic mound out of respect to the assembled multitude. I really did need to go through the fenced-in backyard with a pooper scooper, even if the mess had proven an effective defense against worblatts.

"OK, let's see what we've got, numbers wise," said Grenn. "I count about 50 or 60 [unpronounceables]. How many of us are mystics, Blurg?"

She did a quick head count. "Seventeen."

"Wow," said the great buck with surprised admiration. "I would think 17 [unpronounceable] mystics is almost all we need to do this."

"Am I the only one who can't pronounce that word?" I said. The buck had pronounced it flawlessly.

"Oh, no, it's impossible for *any* human to pronounce it," Seth the Dragon said. "I don't know why that is."

"I believe we have 29 warrior eagles here," said the eagle chief.

"We have only these six bucks here," said the great buck, turning to his fellow antlered white-tailed deer.

"And your mates," said the doe testily, as five other female deer appeared from the woods.

"And us!" cried several fawns, but the young ones were shushed back into the brush.

"And I think we can all count to five," said one of Seth's dragon friends.

"That's a small army," I said.

"But what good can even all of us do against a hurricane powered by the Evil One?" Dejah asked, and all grew quiet except for the gentle sound of the wind chimes in the autumn breeze.

"I have an idea," said Blurg, the [unpronounceable] wizardess.

She outlined her thought.

An excited hubbub broke out as everyone agreed it just might work.

"OK, we have a week before Halloween," said Seth the Dragon. "Let's get busy."

And everyone got busy.

Summer walked up to me then.

"Daddy, what's a laurel and hearty handshake?" she asked plaintively.

Chapter 27
Preparation

It was late in the afternoon before Halloween.

Blurg and her 16 fellow [unpronounceable] wizards and wizardesses stood in the field outside our backyard fence — in part because our field generals had insisted that I continue to neglect my backyard pickup duties until after Halloween.

"I've never seen a worblatt repellent as effective as what your dogs produce naturally," said Seth the Dragon.

This did not disturb Dejah a great deal, but Summer insisted on submitting to a leash and doing her business in the front yard near the road.

"I hope this whole experience teaches you better habits," Summer said one morning out front. "You are a wonderful daddy except for taking care of the backyard."

I digress: Blurg and her colleagues stood in the field outside our backyard fence, waving their hands in complicated patterns and chanting incantations. A huge inter-dimensional portal appeared, and on the other side I could see the field where we had built our house 12 years ago, except it was empty again.

"Is this a time portal?" I asked. "That looks exactly like our property before we dug the first hole."

"No, we just found another dimension where the house didn't get built," Grenn said.

"Why wasn't it built?" I asked.

"You probably don't want to know," he said, and I realized I didn't.

"If the house isn't there, this won't fool anyone," Dejah said.

"The house will be there tomorrow," Blurg said, sweating from the exertion of creating a portal that large, even with all the others helping. "Don't you worry."

In the sky, 29 warrior eagles were practicing formations, including what appeared to be a formidable line of defense facing southwest over the house. They would scatter and then reform the line, scatter again and then reform the line again.

In the field in front of the septic mound, the 12 white-tailed deer practiced a similar maneuver, bracing themselves between an invisible foe and the modest house.

And all around, five dragons patrolled vigilantly in the sky above even the eagles.

"I have to say, it's a little unnerving that we've been making all these preparations and there's no sign of the evil beings that kept popping in and out on that first day," I said as the sun began to set.

"I know what you mean," Grenn said. "It's been quiet."

And then he broke into a huge grin, and he and Blurg said together, "Almost — TOO quiet!!"

I couldn't help it, they laughed so hard I had to join in.

"Make no mistake, the hurricane is still coming and still on schedule," Philbert said. He had been diligently watching the weather channel all this time. He pointed. "Halloween morning, it should appear in the sky to the southwest over there, and then hit this area as a Category 5."

"That would 'consume everything in its path,' just like the prophecy said," Blurg said, "except we will 'be on watch against the Evil One,' also just like the prophecy said."

"Will you be enough?" Summer asked.

"We will have to be," Grenn said. "Good always triumphs over evil in a fair fight."

"WHO SAID ANYTHING ABOUT A FAIR FIGHT?" There suddenly came a voice that sounded like it was coming from everywhere at once. We looked to the southwest and saw the tall giant who had pretended to be the Evil One. He was flanked by his worblatt henchmen, Bellzy, Bub and Clancy.

Before anyone had a chance to say, "Holy cow, the bad guys are here," the giant said, "GET 'EM, BOYS."

Chapter 28
All Hallow's Eve Eve

I noticed something odd right away. As almost five dozen elfin beings, 29 eagles, a dozen white-tailed deer and five dragons rallied against three worblatts and a whatever-he-was, the loudmouthed giant leader reached his long arm toward Summer. And the three worblatts surrounded Dejah as best they could without stepping over the fence into the backyard.

"They're going after the dogs," I said incredulously. And then I repeated angrily, "They're going after the dogs!"

"Then get them inside!" Grenn yelled.

"Right. Come here, Dejah," I said, and the old white dog scampered up the stairs and through the open patio door. "Summer?"

Summer stared at the giant hand reaching down toward her. She looked around the yard. Then she looked at the giant hand reaching down toward her. With all due respect to the 12 white-tailed deer galloping toward the worblatts, Summer looked like a deer caught in headlights.

"SUMMMERRR!" I screamed as the hand began to close around my sweet, gentle, goofy 3-year-old dog.

"COME HERE, LITTLE GIRL," the giant said, closing his fist around Summer and beginning to lift her off the ground.

Have you ever seen five dragons spew flames from their mouths, all directed at an enormous giant's head? We all had to turn our heads away, the fire was so bright.

The giant's hand went limp, Summer dropped three or four feet to the ground and ran like the wind up the stairs and into the house.

The giant's face was still intact, but it was as charred as you might think it would be after dragons breathed fire from five different directions.

"Ow," said the giant, and it was the first time it was not necessary to use all-caps to quote him. He brought his enormous hands to his face as if to make sure it was still there. Yes, he still had a face, but it resembled a marshmallow that got too close to the campfire.

The giant ringleader stumbled backwards, tripped over one of the willow trees, and landed in a sitting position in the big field beyond the trees.

"OW!" he cried, a little more definitively, and then, waving at the worblatts, cried, "EXTERMINATE THEM ALL!"

"Did you see what they did to the boss?" Bellzy said.

"You heard him, let's get busy!" Clancy cried.

But Seth the dragon gave Clancy a prodigious push from behind, and the monster tripped over the fence and landed face first in the backyard.

I hope I have emphasized enough two facts about my backyard. First, I neglected my duty to pick up after my dogs and was encouraged by various magical beings to maintain this neglect until after Halloween. Second, Clancy the worblatt was disgusted and terrified by dog poo to the level of a phobia.

The scream of horror was deafening. Clancy leapt to his feet, ran across the field and into the woods, which led down through a small wetlands and into the waters of Green Bay. We heard an enormous splash from below and Clancy's cries of "Ew! Ew! Ew!" as he washed his face and body in the great bay.

Meanwhile, the assembled little army of [unpronounceables], dragons, eagles and deer swarmed over the two remaining worblatts and the dazed giant, who stumbled and rumbled and retreated through a hastily constructed inter-dimensional portal.

"That was almost too easy," said the eagle chief.

"Worblatts and their ilk are easy to defeat," said Seth the Dragon. "A hurricane is something else."

"This has to work," said Blurg. "There is no other way."

And as the sun set to begin the night before Halloween and a light breeze started to grow stronger, I voiced the only question on my mind.

"Why did they go after the dogs?"

Chapter 29
The whole point of everything

"Why did they go after the dogs?" I repeated. "The first move they made was to reach for the dogs. What's going on?"

Seth sat down in the field next to the great buck, who had mounted the septic mound. The lead eagle fluttered onto the railing on the deck. Grenn and Blurg hopped onto the chair. I stood on the deck, and the dogs sat just inside the open patio door. The melody of the wind chimes was a constant reminder that the wind was rising.

Everyone looked at me like I had entirely missed the point of everything. It was quiet, except for the wind chimes, for a very long moment.

Blurg, the [unpronounceable] wizards, broke the semi-silence.

"Of course they went after the dogs," she said. "That's the whole point of everything."

"What?" I said.

"What?" Dejah said.

"I don't get it," Summer said.

"It's in the prophecy," said the eagle. "In the time of magic there will come a day when the dimensions merge and tongues are unlocked to a human."

"Right, and beware the Evil One and all that," I said. "What does that have to do with the dogs?"

"Whose tongues did you think are unlocked to a human?"

"Well, everyone's," Dejah said. "He couldn't talk to any of you guys before this all started."

A ripple of laughter rippled through the crowd of eagles, deer, dragons and [unpronounceables].

"We talk to humans all the time," the eagle said. "They just don't listen."

"How can that be?" I said. "I never heard you speak before."

"It's a last resort," said the great buck. "When all else fails and it's absolutely necessary, we speak to you with your words. But dogs can only use your words during the Time of Magic."

"That doesn't seem fair," Summer said.

"It probably isn't," said Grenn. "But humans have a wise saying: 'It is what it is.' It might be the only wise saying they ever conjured on their own."

"So only dogs need their tongues unlocked? Why?" I asked.

"We don't need words, most of the time," Dejah said, her eyes lighting up like James Earl Jones realizing that people will come.

All of the magical beings in the field and the yard nodded with approval.

"From the beginning of time, dogs and humans have been able to talk to one another without words," Dejah said. "Oh, you teach us your words and we understand, but we understand each other in ways that transcend the verbal. Ages ago you took us in when we were hungry and cold, and in return we give you happiness and companionship and love without question."

Seth the Dragon nodded. "Evil cannot stand in the face of happiness and companionship and love, so its first instinct is to remove the dogs."

I began to see. Dejah stepped forward onto the deck and looked up at me until I instinctively began to scratch behind her ears.

"Do you remember when my big sister Willow died?" she said. "The bond was broken. There was a visible hole in your heart for months."

"I remember feeling lost and alone. It felt like a hole, but it wasn't visible."

"Oh, it was visible. It still is," Grenn said. "You just don't have the eyes to see."

"It didn't start to heal until you and Mom brought Summer here," Dejah said.

"Who, me?" Summer said.

"Of course, you little goof," I said.

"The evil ones know how powerful that bond is, and so they aim to break the bond whenever they can," said the eagle chief. "And here, at the nexus point of the storm, that bond is the single biggest element of resistance against the triumph of evil.”

"That's why the dogs are the bait in our plan to trap the Evil One," Blurg said.

"Come again?" asked Summer.

Chapter 30
Halloween Hurricane

It was very windy on Halloween morning. The sky to the southwest was as dark as dark could ever be.

"Ready?" I said, standing just inside the house by the patio door.

Sitting patiently by my side were Dejah Thoris Princess of Mars, my 11-year-old, English cream golden retriever who was wise beyond her years, and Summer, my 3-year-old retriever who was still trying to remember what her name was.

"Ready," said Dejah.

"Ready for what?" said Summer, but she added, "Just kidding, Daddy. Let's do this."

I slid open the patio door, and Dejah waddled onto the deck. I followed and looked back. Summer, as always, was standing just inside the threshold as if trying to decide whether to come out.

"Come on," I coaxed. "Come on out."

After I waved her onto the deck two or three times, she stepped outside.

Today, I really couldn't blame her if she was afraid. Even though there were 17 elfin wizards and wizardesses and three or four dozen tiny warriors, nearly 30 eagles, a dozen large deer, and five dragons standing between the deck and the coming storm, we had seen the video from down south, where hurricanes had ravaged large swaths of territory in recent weeks. And this hurricane was not only more powerful than those storms, it was being directed by some sort of supernatural being — the Evil One, if the prophecy was to be believed.

"Don't worry, little one," said Blurg the wizardess, who had to look up to meet Summer's eyes. "We've got this." She and her 16 mystical colleagues had positioned themselves along the outside of the backyard fence, spaced more or less evenly.

"I don't blame you for being scared, sister," Dejah said. "I'm old, I have most of my life behind me, but you have most of your life ahead."

"I'm not scared, I'm just nervous," Summer said. "And stop talking about how old you are."

A bolt of lightning flashed in the sky, and a moment later thunder rocked the land.

"Here it comes," said Grenn.

The great darkness began to descend, and the wind picked up. More lightning, more thunder, and then rain began to fall.

And then a huge face appeared in the sky in front of the storm. It sort of resembled the giant who was the leader of the worblatt crew, and it sort of resembled the little green guy who had teleported Summer and Seth to Red River Park — especially the green monster's smirky smirk.

His voice, however, was very familiar, and it seemed to be coming from everywhere at once.

"THE TIME OF MAGIC IS AT ITS PEAK, AND MY TIME HAS COME AT LAST," said the huge face.

"I thought he said he wasn't really the Evil One," Dejah said uneasily.

"I LIED. IT'S WHAT I DO BEST," said the face. "OF COURSE I AM THE EVIL ONE. PREPARE YOURSELVES FOR ETERNITY."

Summer, Dejah and I stood on the deck facing the oncoming hurricane and the giant green face. Between us and the storm were a dozen determined white-tailed deer, 29 warrior eagles, five dragons and several dozen [unpronounceable] elfin beings, including the 17 wizards and wizardesses who stood along the fence.

I have to admit, as the wind whipped fallen leaves in circles around the yard and rain started falling sideways in the wind, I began to suspect it wasn't going to be enough.

"Oh dear," Dejah said. Summer just whimpered.

Chapter 31
Into the storm

As leaves were ripped off the trees and swirled around us, Dejah lay down on the deck at the top of the stairs. Summer faltered against the wind but remained standing.

"They said we should stand up as long as we can," Summer told her older sister.

"And I did, Sum, but now I must lie down," Dejah said. "When you're 11 years old yourself, you'll understand."

"Just stay out here on the deck, girls," I said. "I'm proud of you both. And I'm with you all the way."

The wind howled. And so did the Evil One.

"YOU CURSED DOGS," the giant face shrieked from the middle of the hurricane. "YOU HUMILIATED MY MINIONS. YOU OBSTRUCTED MY WONDERFUL SORDID PLANS AT EVERY TURN. NO MORE! NO MORE!"

It was mid-morning. It was dark as midnight except for the nanoseconds when lightning flash and the ground shook.

The great buck and his companions galloped out to meet the storm in the big field beyond the willow trees.

Two or three great lightning flashes were followed by two or three great booms of thunder.

As if on cue, the deer broke ranks and bolted into the comparative shelter of the woods.

The Evil One chuckled and pressed on, his eyes fixed on the two dogs on the deck 100 yards away.

Next came the great array of eagles swooping from the trees even as they bent from the wind. In crisp formation 29 warrior eagles dove into the eye of the storm. Just before they reached the giant green face, they dispersed in all directions — almost as if the chaotic retreat had been choreographed.

The Evil One cackled and pushed closer, his eyes focused on the dogs that refused to leave the deck.

Five dragons lifted from the ground, their nostrils steaming, their great tails flicking in anger, their wings catching the wind so they could soar high and dive-bomb the evil force in the center of the tempest — and just before their mighty claws wrapped around the Evil One, they toppled away as if flung by the wind, and even I couldn't tell if they had dropped back on purpose.

Only the five dozen [unpronounceable] elfin warriors stood between us and the storm, with the 17 wizards and wizardesses along the backyard fence frantically waving their hands and arms and chanting the chants that no human could repeat.

Now laughing monstrously and uncontrollably, the Evil One swept the tiny warriors aside and focused his deadly eyes on the human and his canine companions on the deck.

Just before the storm crossed over the backyard fence and slammed into the house, the Evil One could have sworn the dogs and I disappeared. He had no time to register that inkling, because he and his storm slammed into the little blue house and shattered it into 10,000 splinters, flattening the apple trees in the front yard and leveling the forest for miles around.

"AND SO WE SEE THAT ALL I TOUCH WITH MY BEAUTIFUL WICKEDNESS IS DOOMED," the Evil One shouted with a triumphant guffaw.

He turned back to survey the havoc he had wrought, but instead he saw the little blue house still standing, untouched on the other side of the huge inter-dimensional portal that the little mystics had generated for the storm to pass through.

And just as the monster cried, "WHAT HAVE THEY DONE?!" the 17 little [unpronounceables] performed the special gestures and incantations that closed the portal again with a rather unpleasant zipping sound.

Chapter 32
Halloween sunset

Grenn and Blurg clinked their glasses of mead together and drank heartily. The fawns scampered around the field chasing each other's tails, and the eagles practiced aerial maneuvers that would challenge Blue Angels.

Seth the Dragon rested his head on the deck railing and smiled at the two golden retrievers who looked up at him.

"I got to tell you, as hard as it was trying to realistically fake being tossed away by a little wind, I have to admire how you two just stood there calmly being the bait for our trap," Seth told them.

"I was not calm," Summer admitted.

"I must admit, we were offended when it was suggested my forces pretend to be scattered by the wind," said the eagle chief. "But the ruse served its purpose."

"We had to keep the Evil One distracted so he wouldn't notice the little ones conjuring at the fence," Seth said.

"I'm just glad our [unpronounceable] friends came through with the spell that created a fake house on the other side of that inter-dimensional portal they conjured," Dejah said. "It looked just like the real thing."

"A perfect target," Seth agreed.

We spent Halloween night reliving the unusual events of this year's Time of Magic and laughing at the TV meteorologists who were flummoxed by the sudden disappearance of the world's worst hurricane seconds after it made landfall from 60,000 feet onto a little plot of land in Northeast Wisconsin. They were calling it a climate change miracle — one or two called it magic and didn't realize how right they were.

Around midnight the party started breaking up and the feathered and fur-clad friends we had met in recent weeks started to head to their own homes.

"It has been a pleasure to serve with you," said the great buck. "Perhaps 'pleasure' is the wrong word. It's been an honor."

"The honor is ours," I said.

"Thank you for your help," Dejah said.

"And be careful next month," Summer said. "Deer season is coming."

"Don't remind me," the buck said with a grim chuckle, and then he and his family had disappeared into the night.

"You comported yourself with dignity and pride," the chief eagle said as he said his own farewells. Before we could respond, he was gone, too.

Seth said goodbye to his four fellow dragons and then turned to us.

"My kind doesn't really show itself outside the Time of Magic," the big dragon said. "Nothing personal, we just don't like to freak people out, despite our reputation."

"Well, you never freak out [unpronounceables]," Grenn said, "so don't be a stranger around our house."

"You got it," Seth said. "And Dejah and Summer, consider yourself honorary dragons. You did good when the chips were down."

Without another word, and with a flourish of his mighty wings, the dragon lifted into the sky and disappeared.

"He didn't give me time to say thank you," I said.

"We'll pass the word along," said Blurg, taking Grenn's hand, which confirmed my suspicion that she and the stalwart little leader were an item.

"I'm sorry we infringed on your land when we built the house," I told them. "I hope we can be friends anyway."

"Ah, there's a lot of land to go around, and we don't need that much space," Grenn said. "You didn't realize how rude you were being."

"There's that," Dejah said.

"Don't be a stranger," I said.

"Well, it's kind of a tradition that we only make ourselves seen during the Time of Magic," Grenn said.

"But we'll make a point of dropping by next October if not sooner."

"What about the Evil One? Is he stuck in that other dimension now?" Summer asked.

"Listen, little girl, when my crew zips up an inter-dimensional portal, it stays zipped until we say otherwise," Blurg said. "Don't you worry."

"I guess this is goodbye for now," I said. "October is just about over."

"Yep, see you when next we see you," Grenn said. "And thanks for everything. I'll leave you three to say your last words to each other."

"Last words?" Summer asked.

"Well, after the magic fades, your Daddy won't be able to understand what you're saying again until next year around this time."

Dejah and Summer and I looked at each other.

"Oh," Dejah said.

Chapter 33
The magic fades

As the elfin beings entered the woods and were no longer visible, I looked at my two golden retrievers, who had bravely faced down the storm and weathered the adventure like the heroines they were. What do you say when you won't be able to speak to each other for another year?

"Dejah, Summer, I just have to say —" I began, sitting down on an easy chair.

"No, you don't," Dejah said, resting her head on the arm. "This is our time to talk. We understand you just fine all the time, but we won't be able to tell you anything with words."

"So you do understand me all the time?" I said, a little smile forming. "So when I say, 'Summer, come in the house,' you're just refusing?"

"Well, sometimes I don't wanna," Summer said with a rueful look.

"The Time of Magic is almost over, so let me say something, or several somethings," said my 11-year-old puppy. "Thank you."

"Well, you're welcome, Dejah," I said. "I'm sorry you had to play second fiddle for most of your life. First, there was Willow, and then you ruled the roost for only five months before we brought Summer home."

Dejah smiled the way only golden retrievers can smile.

"Anyone could see that Willow was the best dog who ever lived, and everyone loves the puppy best, even when it's a goof like Summer," Dejah said.

"Hey!" Summer said, but they both wagged their tails.

"And you and Mom gave me plenty of puppy love back in the day," Dejah continued. "Anyway, the second fiddle is still a darn good player, and you never treated me like anything less than one of the two best dogs there are."

"Well, you are," I said, "and you were Mom's puppy. I'm so sorry Mom had to leave."

"It wasn't your fault, and it wasn't her fault. She got sick and then she died. You told us," Summer said. "We know. We always knew."

We were all silent for a little while.

And then Dejah said, "So thank you. This probably is the last time I'll be able to say the words so you can hear them, so I want to say it now. You've always taken care of me and made me feel loved."

"Of course you're loved, you little goombah," I said, surprised that I could speak at all because I sure couldn't see through the watery film. "In any case, we'll pick up this conversation next October, when the Time of Magic rolls around again."

Dejah looked at me with compassion. "Daddy," she said, "you've never had a 12-year-old golden retriever."

I knew what she was saying, and I refused to hear.

"Well, maybe you'll be the first," I said. "You're a pretty feisty old broad."

"You two are so serious," Summer said. "Let's play!" And suddenly she ran from the love seat to the kitchen and back to the love seat and back to the kitchen and back to the love seat and into my office and back to the kitchen and back to the love seat.

"Do you know there's a word for that, you goof?" I said.

"A word for what?" Summer said, panting.

"Zoomie. You just did a zoomie."

"I like that word! Zoomie!" she shouted, and did a few more rounds around the living room.

Dejah shook her head. "Kids."

In a little while I climbed into bed, and Summer jumped up near my feet, and Dejah settled in the doorway to the bedroom, our usual positions.

"Thanks for the adventure, girls," I said. "I love you."

"Wouldn't miss it for the world," Dejah said without lifting her head as she sprawled in the doorway. "We love you, too."

"What she said, Daddy," said Summer, the kind and gentle but shy big puppy.

The room went quiet, and soon the three of us were dreaming of dragons and eagles and white-tailed deer and [unpronounceables].

Epilogue

And now it was November.

I awoke to the song of the wind chimes dancing in a brisk breeze, and I was alarmed for a moment before I remembered the hurricane danger was over.

"It's just a plain old gale of November, right, Sum?" I said.

"Woof," said Summer.

"That's right," I said, a little sadly. "You're just a dog again."

She tilted her head as if to say, "What do you mean, *just* a dog?" I laughed and rubbed her head, then I wrapped her in a big morning bear hug.

Summer squirmed free and ran to the patio door, where Dejah was already whining.

"I know, old dog, what took me so long?" I said, sliding the door open. The 11-year-old dashed outside and down the steps to the yard, and I stepped outside. Summer, as usual, hesitated just inside the house.

I laughed and stretched my arms out.

"Oh, come on, Sum," I said. "It's a good day to have a good day! And the worblatts are gone, there are leaves all over the ground to play in, and we'll probably never spot him but there's a dragon around here somewhere watching over the land."

At that, the 3-year-old's ears perked up, and she came outside and ran down the stairs. She looked back up at me.

I sighed. "I'll be right down, girl."

Stepping back into the house briefly, I grabbed two or three supermarket plastic bags out of the pantry, brought them out and closed the patio door. I walked down to the yard and grabbed the pooper scooper.

Her business finished, Dejah went up and lay down at the top of the stairs to enjoy the morning while I policed the yard and Summer did zoomies in the sun.

Afterword

It was the last week in September 2024 when I wrote a blog post called "The adventure begins," and on the spur of the moment, an adventure began.

I had no intention to write a second chapter. It was just a little bit of flash fiction about a morning when Dejah, my beloved 11-year-old golden retriever, started talking to me. Like most flash fiction, it was just a burst of creativity meant to get the reader wondering what might happen next, the shortest of short stories.

I sat in my writing chair thinking about what to write for the next day's blog post, and my mind kept drifting back to the unpleasant presidential campaign. I had no desire to add fuel to those flames. But oh, the temptation to weigh in on the ongoing puppet theater. What else could I write about with everyone screaming in my ears about politics and government?

And then I thought, what if I forced myself to write something else? What if I boxed myself into a writing project that would take me past the election?

On a whim I decided to write a second chapter. And the next day, I wrote a third, introducing an elf-like being who happened to live in the neighborhood. Before long the story was unfolding, with dragons and eagles and more elfin beings the name of whose race humans can't pronounce. I gave myself one rule: Each chapter would begin by resolving the previous day's cliffhanger, something weird would happen, and there would be another cliffhanger.

Before I knew it, the month had gone by and I had a novella, which — unless you're one of those people who reads the afterword first — you have just finished. Believe me, I had more fun this October than I would have if I had left writing about the election as one of my daily options. I hope you did, too.

Along the way I discovered a way to do something I had been trying to do for years: Make a habit out of writing a little bit of fiction every day. If I keep up this new habit, maybe I'll finally finish some of those novels I have lying around the house in various states of undone.

One thing at a time. For now, I hope you enjoyed my little Halloween hurricane story. You can follow my daily blog posts at warrenbluhm.com and/or support my efforts at Patreon.

But if you'll excuse me now, Dejah is whining at the patio door to go out again.

Warren Bluhm

Nov. 8, 2024